DOUG SAVAGE

Andrews McMeel
PUBLISHING®

for Mom

Thanks for so many things, but especially for encouraging us to read, to be creative, and to be resilient and brave in the face of life's evil supervillains.

CONTENTS

NOT COOL, MAN.

PART 1:
DISCO AVALANCHE
HELLO, LASER MOOSE!
HELLO, RABBIT BOY!

WHY ARE YOU WHISPERING?
SHHH!

I'M ON THE TRAIL OF A DANGEROUS SUPERVILLAIN!

REALLY? CAN I HELP?

I DON'T KNOW. THINGS COULD GET A LITTLE DANGEROUS—

LET'S GO!

WELL ACTUALLY, HE'S RIGHT OVER THERE, ON THE OTHER SIDE OF THIS FIELD.

WHERE?

RIGHT... OVER...

THERE.

OH!

I'VE BEEN TRACKING THIS GUY FOR THREE DAYS. HE IS EXTREMELY DANGEROUS.

OH MY!

LOOKS PRETTY EVIL, HUH?

THAT'S ONE SCARY-LOOKING WOLF!

?

THE WOLF?? YOU MEAN GUS??

THE BIG SCARY WOLF IS CALLED "GUS"?

HA! GUS ISN'T SCARY! GUS IS A GOOD GUY!

I THOUGHT YOU SAID HE WAS EVIL?

NO, NO. I'M NOT TALKING ABOUT GUS!
I'M TALKING ABOUT THE GUY NEXT TO GUS.

WHAT GUY?
THAT GUY.

UM... THE CHICKADEE?

YES. THAT CHICKADEE IS PURE EVIL.

BUT CHICKADEES ARE THE CUTEST BIRDS EVER!
CUTE, YES. BUT...

THIS ONE IS EVIL.

AN ADORABLE BUT COMPLETELY EVIL LITTLE CHICKADEE.

I DON'T BELIEVE IT.
WHY NOT? YOU'VE MET EVIL CREATURES BEFORE. LIKE CYBORGUPINE.

YEAH BUT CHICKADEES ARE SO LITTLE... AND THEY LOOK LIKE THEY HAVE LITTLE HATS AND GOATEES. THEY'RE SO CUTE!

THIS PARTICULAR CHICKADEE IS QUITE SINISTER, I ASSURE YOU.
WELL THAT'S RIDICULOUS.

♫ IT'S A DISCO AVALANCHE ♫
Stuart's
DISCO
SUPPLIES

♫ THE GROOVE IS ROLLING DOWN
Stuart's
DISCO
SUPPLIES

♫ AND YOU KNOW YOU'VE GOTTA DANCE ♫

♪ GOTTA GET OUT ON THE TOWN ♫

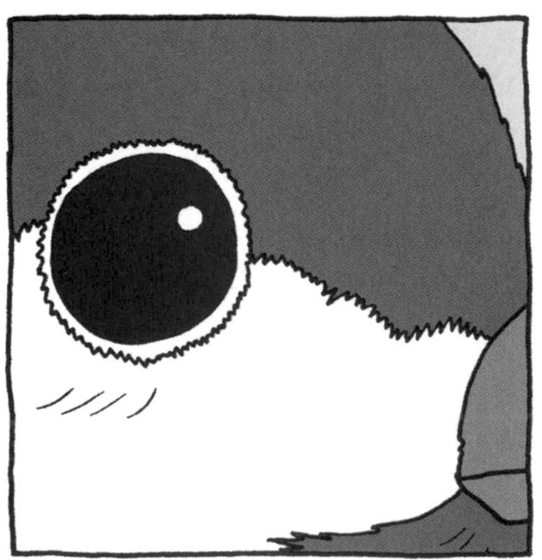

CHICKADEE-DEE-DEE!

PECK!

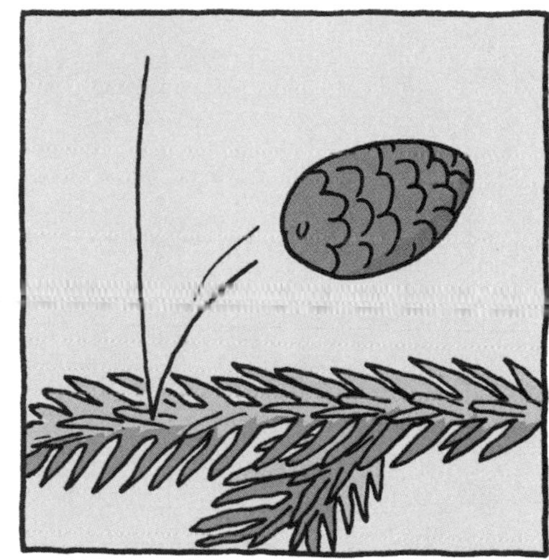

BONK!

OOF!
YAY!

!
SNAP!

SPROING!

AAAUUUGH!

AAAAUGH!

HUH?

THUP!
!

SCREEE

SCREEE

♫ THE BEAT IS GETTING FASTER ♪ IT'S A DISCO AVALANCHE ♫

♫ IT'S A NATURAL DISASTER ♪ IT'S A DISCO AVALA—
SHFLUNK!

SCREECH
Stuart's
DISCO
SUPPLIES

CLICK!

SCREEECH!
Stuart's
DISCO
SUPPLIES

DISCO BALLS
DISCO BALLS
DISCO BALLS

BUMP!

Stuart's
DISCO
SUPPLIES

DISCO BALLS
DISCO BALLS
DISCO BALLS
DISCO BALLS

DISCO BALLS
HUNDREDS OF MIRRORS!
MAKE YOUR PARTY GROOVY WITH THE ULTIMATE DISCO LIGHT SHOW!

SMASH

I'M SORRY, I JUST CAN'T IMAGINE A SWEET LITTLE CHICKADEE BEING EVIL. I NEED PROOF BEFORE—

SCREEEEEE!

WHAT WAS THAT?

IT SOUNDED LIKE AN EAGLE GETTING A SPIDER IN THE FACE.
BUT THAT CAN'T BE... UNLESS... LET'S GO!

SCREEE!

!
PONK!
CRACK!
PONK!

SMASH!

LOOK OUT!

THUNK!

OKAY. THAT'S IT.
ZZZT!
ZZZT!
TIME TO PUT A STOP TO THESE THINGS.

ZZZT!
ZZZT!

PSH!
OW!

MY LASERS! THOSE THINGS ARE REFLECTING MY LASERS!

THEY'RE COVERED WITH TINY MIRRORS!

TIME FOR PLAN B!
WHAT'S PLAN B?

RUN!
SMASH!
RUNNING IS ALWAYS PLAN B.
MAYBE WE SHOULD MAKE IT PLAN A FROM NOW ON?

IT'S OKAY! LOOK!

THEY'VE STOPPED!

WHAT ARE THESE THINGS?

HMM...

WHATEVER THEY ARE, THEY'RE DANGEROUS.

AND I THINK EVIL CHICKADEE IS RESPONSIBLE FOR THIS MESS.

WHAT? HOW COULD A CUTE LITTLE BIRD DO ALL OF THIS?

THAT'S RIDICULOUS!

RIDICULOUS, MAYBE.
BUT I KNOW I'M RIGHT.

HEY! I REMEMBER WHERE I'VE SEEN THESE MIRROR BALLS BEFORE!

WHERE?

IN MY "LASERS AND YOU" BOOK!
LASERS AND YOU
THERE'S A PICTURE OF ONE IN MY BOOK. THEY'RE FOR DANCING!

DANCING?
THAT MAKES NO SENSE.

NO, NO, IT'S TRUE!

THERE'S A SECTION IN THE BOOK ABOUT USING LASERS FOR LIGHT SHOWS. WHEN HUMANS GO DANCING, THEY GO TO SPECIAL BUILDINGS, CALLED "DISCOS."

DISCOS?

YES, AND THESE BALLS ARE USED TO REFLECT LASERS AND OTHER LIGHTS AROUND THE ROOM.
WHY?

THEY'RE PRETTY! I THINK IT MAKES PEOPLE WANT TO DANCE!

WHAT ARE YOU DOING?

I'M DANCING! RABBITS ARE NATURAL DANCERS.

I THOUGHT THAT RABBITS JUST LIKED TO HOP?
THE HOP IS JUST ONE OF THE DANCES WE LIKE TO DO.

WELL, YOU LOOK RIDICULOUS.
THIS IS WHY MOOSE DO NOT DANCE.
YOU SHOULD TRY IT!

DANCING IS FUN

IT'S LIKE SMILING...

WITH YOUR WHOLE BODY!

I'LL TAKE YOUR WORD FOR IT. BUT THERE'S NOTHING FUN ABOUT THESE THINGS.

LOOK, I'LL SHOW YOU—
NO!

ZZZT!

ZZZT!

ZZZT!
AUGH!
ZZZT!

OOPS.
SORRY, FRANK!

IT'S NOT THAT NOTICEABLE, FRANK!

GRUMBLE GRUMBLE

FRANK?

YEAH, THESE DISCO BALLS ARE PRETTY DANGEROUS.

LET'S HIDE THEM IN THOSE REEDS.

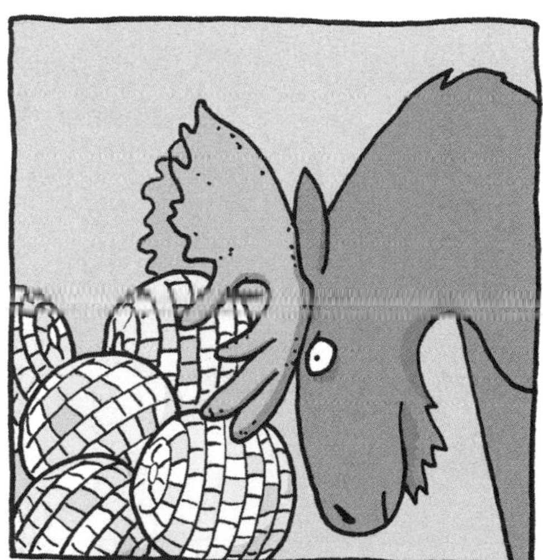

THERE. SAFELY HIDDEN.

INTERESTING.

TWO MONTHS LATER...

PART 2:
A MOOSE WITHOUT LASERS

SLAM!
CLICK!

CLICK!

PSSH!

SHINEX

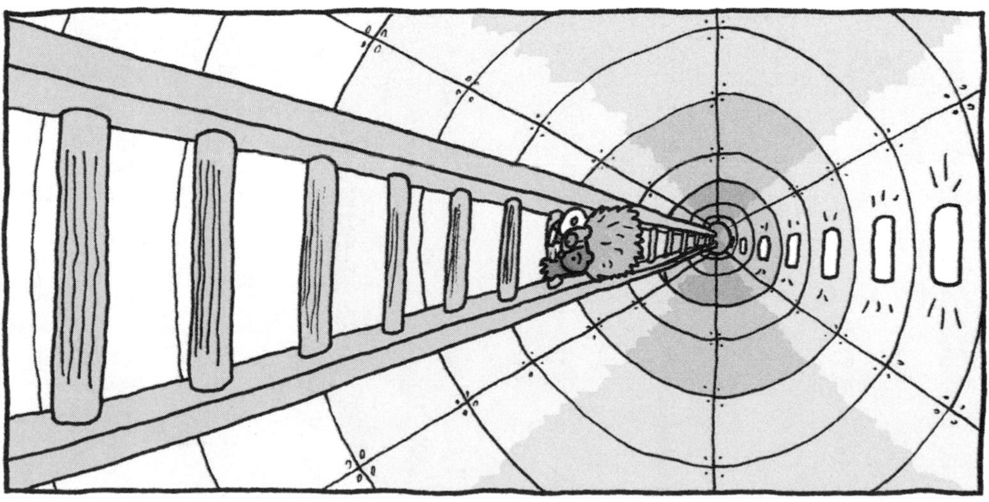

CAVE, SWEET CAVE!

TOXICORP

SPTZ!
SHINEX

WIPE!

THERE! IT'S READY.

TIME FOR A TEST DRIVE!

STOMP
STOMP

IS THIS THE PLACE?

YES, I WAS EATING A PATCH OF CLOVER OVER THERE AND I LOOKED UP AND HE WAS ON THAT TREE, STARING AT ME.

THEN HE SAID "CHICKADEE" AND FLEW AWAY.

IT'S PRETTY CLOSE TO WHERE WE SAW HIM BEFORE...

THIS MUST BE HIS HUNTING GROUND.

"HUNTING GROUND"? YOU KNOW, I'M STILL NOT CONVINCED THAT HE'S EVIL.

HE MIGHT BE A LITTLE WEIRD. BUT HE'S JUST A CUTE LITTLE CHICKADEE.

CUTE AS A BUTTON, YES.

BUT NOT CUTE ON THE INSIDE.

BUT HAVE YOU ACTUALLY SEEN HIM DO ANYTHING EVIL?

UM... NO. BUT BAD THINGS HAPPEN WHENEVER HE'S AROUND.

IT'S NO COINCIDENCE.

BUT YOU CAN'T JUST SHOOT HIM WITH LASERS BECAUSE YOU THINK HE'S EVIL, RIGHT?

I KNOW THAT EVIL CHICKADEE IS EVIL.
WHEN YOU'VE BEEN PROTECTING THE FOREST AS LONG AS I HAVE, YOU GET A SENSE OF THESE THINGS.

BUT YOU NEED PROOF, RIGHT?

YES, I SUPPOSE I NEED PROOF.

WE NEED TO KNOW HE HAS COMMITTED A CRIME.

CHICKADEE.

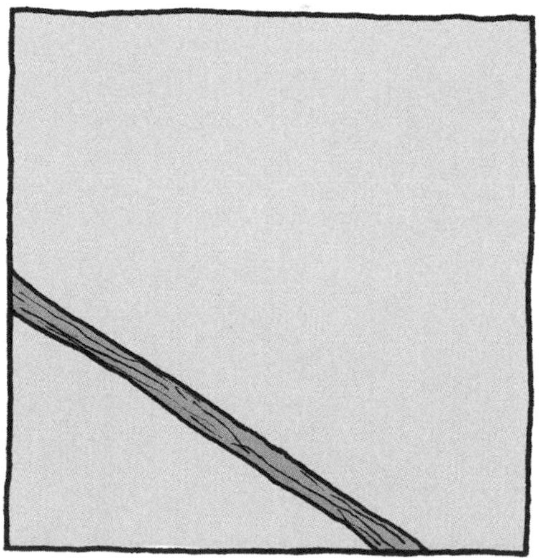

NOM NOM NOM NOM

CHICKADEE!

PONK!

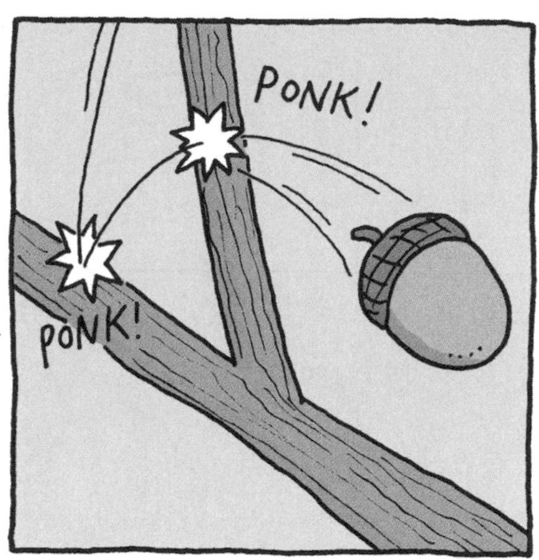
PONK!
PONK!

SMACK!

YEOW!

ZZZZT!
CHOP!
ZZZT!
ZZZT!

ZZZZT!
LASER MOOSE!

IT'S OKAY!

IT'S JUST A SQUIRREL!

OH! SORRY, THAT REALLY STARTLED ME.

WHAT A CLUMSY SQUIRREL!

OH, NO, HE WASN'T CLUMSY. EVIL CHICKADEE IS RESPONSIBLE FOR THIS.

I HEARD HIM YELL, JUST BEFORE THE SQUIRREL FELL.
HE MUST KNOW THAT I'M COMING FOR HIM.

YOU HEARD HIM YELL?

YES, HE YELLED "CHICKADEE."

DON'T ALL CHICKADEES YELL "CHICKADEE"?

YES. BUT THIS SOUNDED MORE MENACING.

I DON'T KNOW. I STILL HAVE TROUBLE BELIEVING THAT A CHICKADEE CAN BE A SUPERVILLAIN.

SUPERVILLAINS SHOULD BE STRONGER AND SCARIER AND MORE DANGEROUS—
LIKE THIS?

BEHOLD! MY DISCO BATTLE SUIT!

PREPARE TO DIE!

WAIT! LASER MOOSE! HE'S COVERED IN—

-MIRRORS!

HA!

CHOP!

HA! YOU CAN'T TOUCH ME, LASER MOOSE!

GASH!
AUGH!

RABBIT BOY!
I CAN'T USE MY LASERS! HIS SUIT REFLECTS THEM!
I DON'T KNOW WHAT TO DO!
I'LL TELL YOU WHAT TO DO, LASER MOOSE.
GIVE UP!

SMACK!

CRACK!
CRUNCH!

POP!

GOODBYE, LASER MOOSE!

CRACK
HUH?
GET OUT OF HERE, YOU LITTLE PUNK!
SWIPE!
OW!

WE SHOULD GET OUT OF HERE.

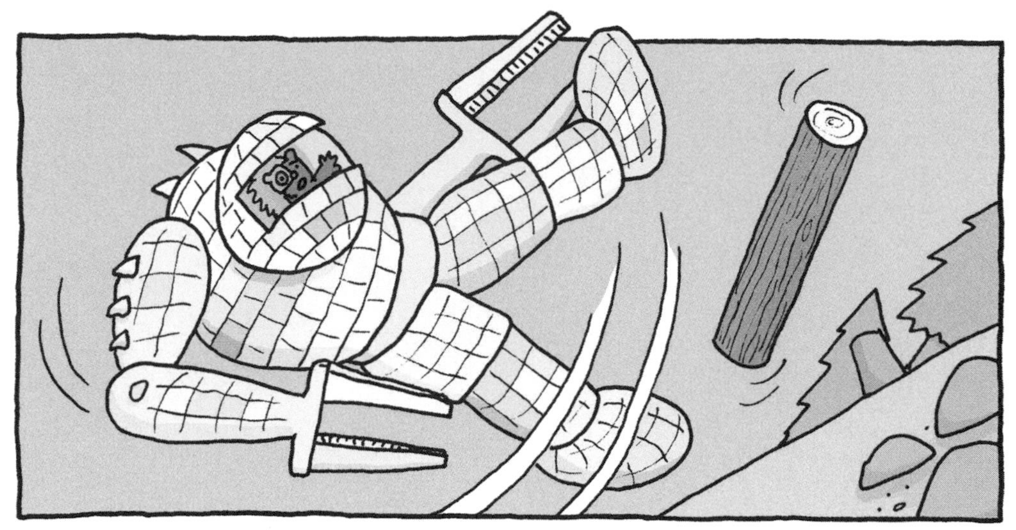

THUD

UG...

HE'S GONE!
ARRGH!!!

ARGH!!

IT DOESN'T SOUND LIKE HE'S CHASING US.

FOR NOW.

BUT HE WILL. HE WON'T REST UNTIL HE DESTROYS ME.

WHO AM I, RABBIT BOY?
YOU'RE LASER MOOSE, OF COURSE!

AM I? I CAN'T USE MY LASERS TO FIGHT CYBORGUPINE.
AND A MOOSE WITHOUT LASERS IS... JUST A MOOSE.

WELL, THAT'S CRAZY TALK.

YOU'RE NOT JUST A MOOSE. YOU'RE A HERO. AND YOU DON'T NEED LASERS TO BE A HERO.

YOU ALWAYS GO OUT OF YOUR WAY TO HELP OTHERS.

YOU ALWAYS FIGHT THE FORCES OF EVIL!

AND NOBODY ASKED YOU TO DO IT. YOU DO IT BECAUSE IT'S THE RIGHT THING TO DO!

I DON'T KNOW IF I CAN DEFEAT CYBORGUPINE AND HIS DISCO SUIT.

HE'S TOO STRONG. AND WITHOUT LASERS, I MIGHT AS WELL BE THROWING STICKS AT HIM.

THEN WE'LL THROW STICKS AT HIM!
BESIDES, YOU'VE GOT MORE THAN JUST LASERS!
YOU'VE GOT SMARTS! YOU'VE GOT STUBBORN DETERMINATION!

I'M NOT STUBBORN!

OKAY, THEN YOU'VE GOT REGULAR NON-STUBBORN DETERMINATION.

AND YOU'VE GOT FRIENDS.

WE CAN DO THIS TOGETHER. WE JUST NEED TO THINK CREATIVELY.

AND BESIDES, YOU'RE LASER MOOSE. <YAWN!> YOU CAN DO ANYTHING YOU SET YOUR MIND TO.

THANKS, RABBIT BOY.

YOU'RE RIGHT.
I'M LASER MOOSE.
I CAN DO ANYTHING
I SET MY MIND TO.

PART 3:
DISCO FEVER

OW!
PLUCK!

LIQUID
SLEEP

LIQUID
SLEEP

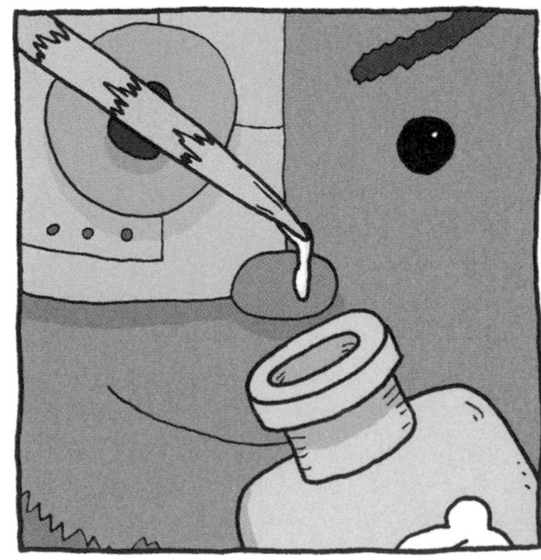

I'LL HAVE TO GET HIM TO COME TO ME.

BRAIN
SURGERY
AND YOU

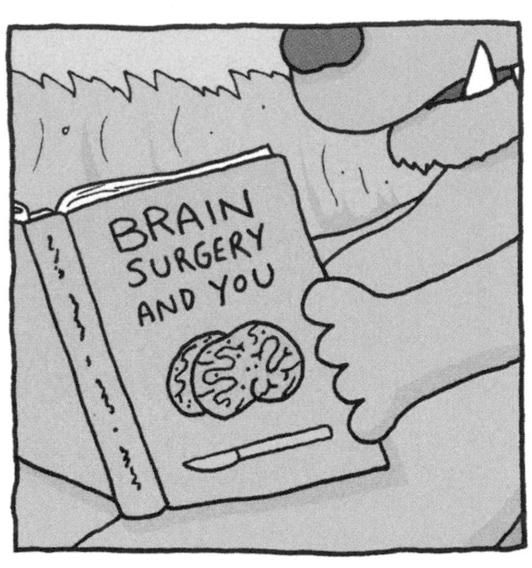
BRAIN
SURGERY
AND YOU

!
SHTOOK!

WHAT THE—

ZZZZZZZ

YUM!

FToo!

HEY!
SHTOOK!

ZZZZ

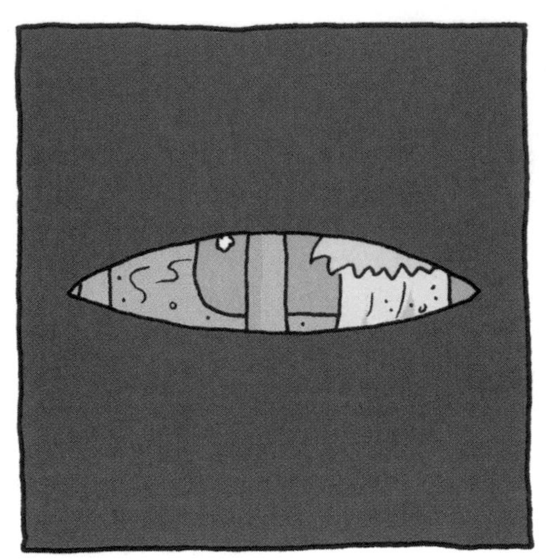

HUH? WHERE AM I?

AUGH! HELP! I'M TRAPPED IN A CAGE WITH A WOLF!

HA! DON'T WORRY ABOUT ME.
I'M A VEGETARIAN.

BESIDES, BEING TRAPPED IN A CAGE ISN'T OUR WORST PROBLEM RIGHT NOW.

BEING TRAPPED IN A CAGE THAT IS SLOWLY SINKING INTO THE MUD... NOW THAT'S A PROBLEM!

AUGH! HELP! SOMEBODY, HELP!

HELP!

THIS IS IT. LET'S GO!
BUT OUR PLAN ISN'T READY!

WELL IT'S GOING TO HAVE TO BE READY ENOUGH.

HELP!!!

LASER MOOSE! HELP! WE'RE GOING TO DROWN!
STAY BACK! IT'S A TRAP!

POK

OW.

LASER MOOSE! REMEMBER THE PLAN!

MWAHAHAHA!!!

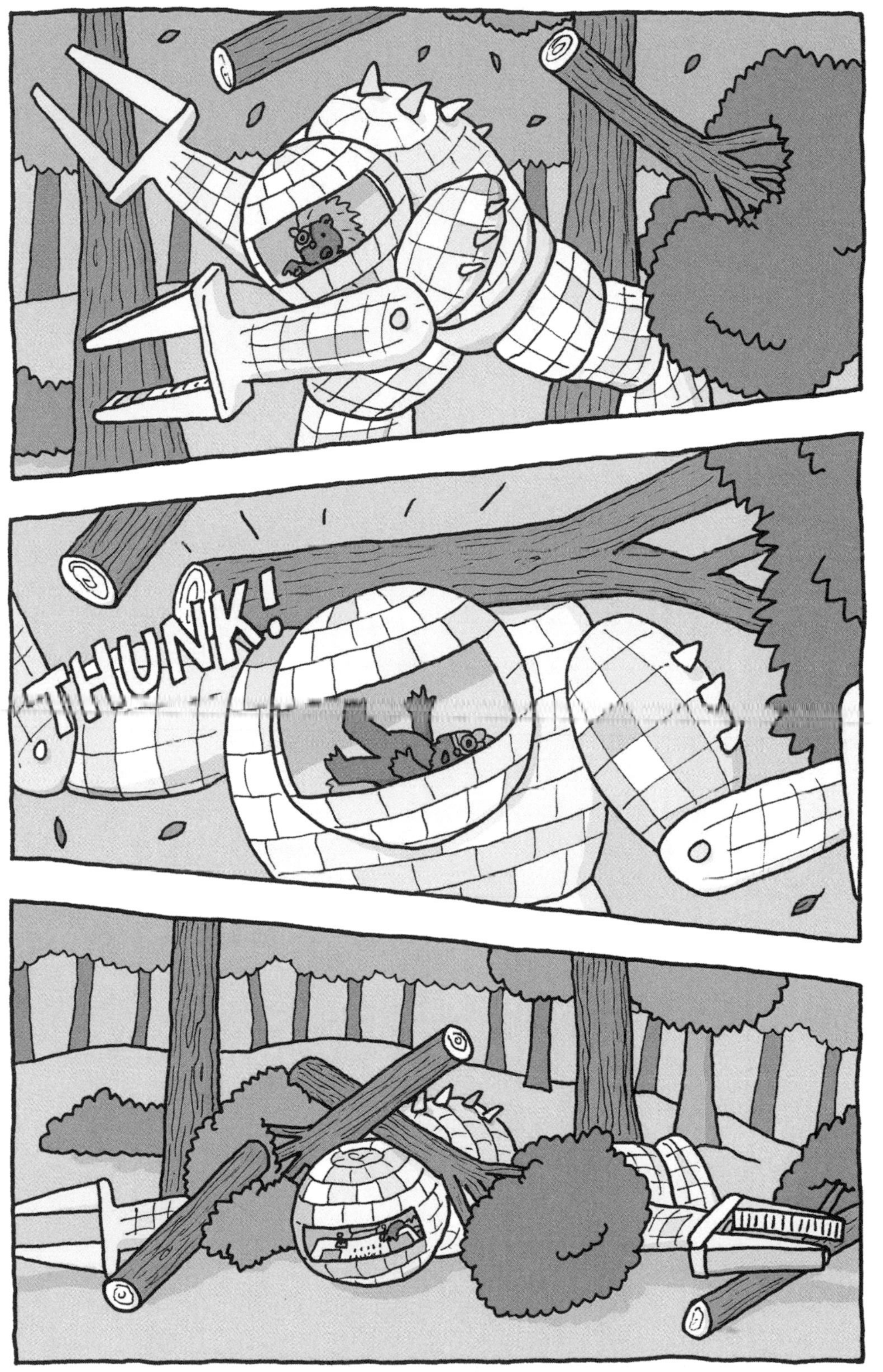
THUNK!

HA! TAKE THAT, VILLAIN!

LASER MOOSE! COME QUICK!

LET'S GET YOU GUYS
OUT OF THERE.

LOOK
OUT!

RUMBLE
RUMBLE

SNAP!
SNAP!
ARE YOU AFRAID TO FIGHT ME, LASER MOOSE?

LET'S DO THIS.

GLUB!

YOU GUYS OKAY?
WE'LL BE ALRIGHT. THANKS, RABBIT BOY.

?
BLAST!
WHAT?!

HOW'S IT GOING?

THE PLAN IS WORKING!

SHOOT LASERS AT EVERYTHING THAT ISN'T A MIRROR?
YEP.

NICE. THEN WHAT?
I DON'T KNOW. WE DIDN'T EXACTLY FINISH THE PLAN.

UH OH! HE'S GETTING UP AGAIN!

THEN I'D BETTER KNOCK HIM DOWN AGAIN!

ZZZT!

GASH!

CRACK!

OUCH.

EVIL CHICKADEE?! WHAT IS HE DOING HERE?

RABBIT BOY, YOU KEEP AN EYE ON EVIL CHICKADEE. I'LL TAKE CARE OF CYBORGUPINE.

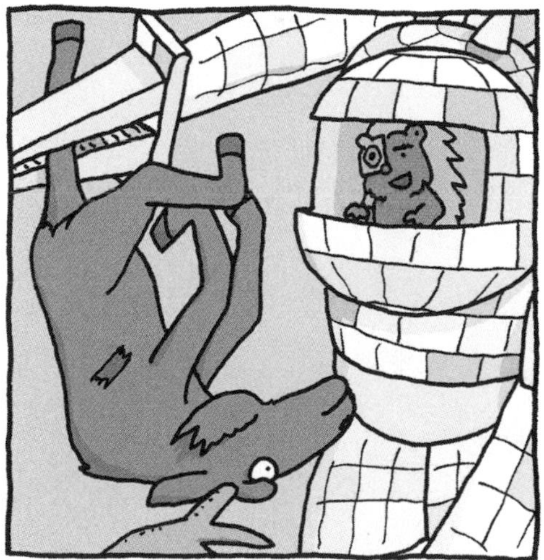

STOP THIS, CYBORGUPINE. THIS IS YOUR FINAL WARNING.
"MY FINAL WARNING"? HA! GOODBYE, LASER MOOSE.

THIS IS NOT HOW I IMAGINED THIS DAY WAS GOING TO GO.

CHICKADEE!

FRANK!

FRANK!
WATCH OUT!
ABOVE YOU!

WHAT?

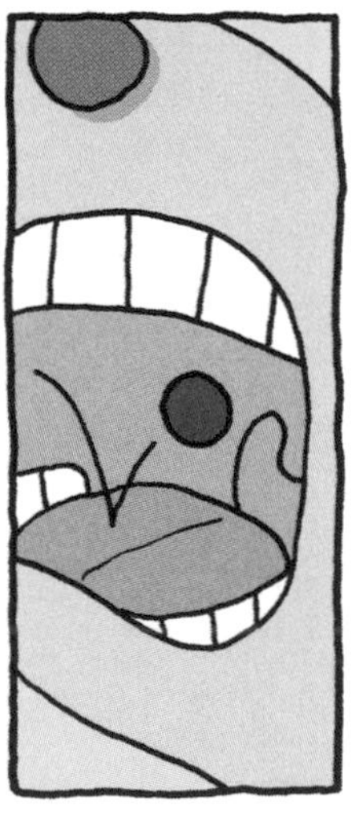

GAK!

FRANK?
GAK
GAK

GAK
GAK

OOF!

COUGH!

PLINK!

SNAP!

RUMBLE

CHICKADEE.
WATCH OUT!
CRACK!

SMACK

SPLORSH!

GLURP!

AS YOU CAN SEE, LASER MOOSE, MY DISCO SUIT IS INDESTRUCTIBLE!

CHOP!

NOOOO!

CYBORGUPINE! DID YOU SAY "INDESTRUCTIBLE"?

AUGH! MY MIRRORS ARE TOO DIRTY TO REFLECT LASERS!

I'VE GOT TO RINSE THIS MUD OFF OF MY SUIT!

!
!

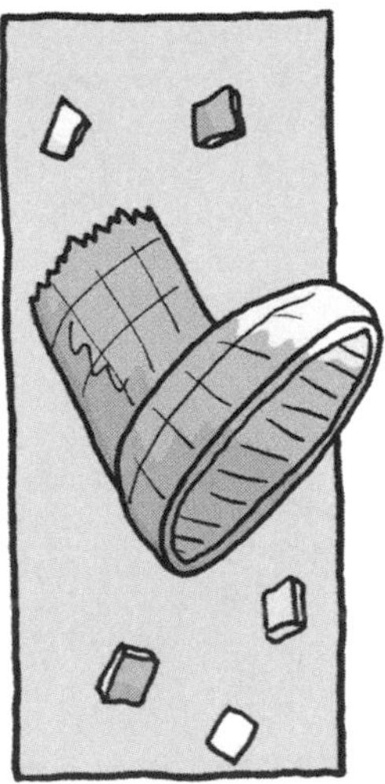

ZZZZT!

ZZ-ZT!

SMACK

SO LONG, CYBORGUPINE!

I'LL GET YOU FOR THIS—
OOF!
LASER MOOSE!

...CHICKADEE...
?

AHA! YOU'RE TRAPPED, EVIL CHICKADEE. AND MY LASERS WILL PUT A STOP TO YOUR REIGN OF TERROR!

WAIT! YOU STILL DON'T KNOW IF EVIL CHICKADEE IS TRULY EVIL.
WHAT IF HE REALLY DID DO ALL OF THOSE THINGS BY MISTAKE? WE CAN'T KNOW FOR CERTAIN!

AND WHAT ABOUT THE BOULDER?

YOU MEAN THE BOULDER THAT HE TRIED TO CRUSH ME WITH?

OR THAT HE TRIED TO SAVE YOU WITH? MAYBE HE MEANT TO HIT CYBORGUPINE? MAYBE EVIL CHICKADEE IS ON YOUR SIDE?

OR MAYBE HE MASTERMINDED THIS ENTIRE THING FROM THE BEGINNING, KNOWING THAT IT COULD LEAD TO MY DESTRUCTION?

!
ZZZT!

YOU LET HIM GO!
?

YOU WERE RIGHT. EVEN THOUGH I KNOW IT IN MY BONES, I CAN'T BE 100% CERTAIN THAT EVIL CHICKADEE IS EVIL. SO WE MUST SET HIM FREE.

SOMETIMES THE MOST HEROIC THING YOU CAN DO IS GIVE SOMEBODY A SECOND CHANCE.

YOU'RE RIGHT, RABBIT BOY.
AND YOU'RE REALLY CHEESY. BUT YOU'RE RIGHT.

SHALL WE GO WATCH OUT FOR MORE DANGER?
WELL, WITH ALL OF THIS NICE DISCO LIGHT, I THINK IT MIGHT BE A GOOD TIME TO TEACH YOU HOW TO DANCE!

HA! I TOLD YOU. MOOSE DO NOT DANCE.

I THOUGHT YOU SAID YOU COULD DO ANYTHING THAT YOU SET YOUR MIND TO?

YES I CAN DO ANYTHING I SET MY MIND TO!

PROVE IT!
I WILL!

HEY THIS IS PRETTY FUN!

GO, LASER MOOSE!

MORE TO EXPLORE!
Learn About DANCING!

DID YOU KNOW THAT DANCING IS ACTUALLY GOOD FOR YOUR BRAIN?

BUT IT'S ALL ABOUT MOVING YOUR FEET!

IT DOESN'T LOOK LIKE IT HAS MUCH TO DO WITH YOUR HEAD!

BUT IT'S TRUE! DANCING HELPS YOUR BRAIN'S SENSE OF BALANCE...
AND DANCING IMPROVES YOUR BRAIN'S ABILITY TO PROCESS COMPLEX MOVEMENTS.

AND RESEARCH SHOWS THAT DANCING ALSO HELPS WITH NEUROPLASTICITY.
NEURO-WHAT?

NEUROPLASTICITY. IT'S A FANCY WORD THAT MEANS THAT, THROUGHOUT YOUR LIFE, THE LITTLE BITS OF YOUR BRAIN ARE GOOD AT LEARNING NEW WAYS TO CONNECT TO THE OTHER LITTLE BITS OF YOUR BRAIN.

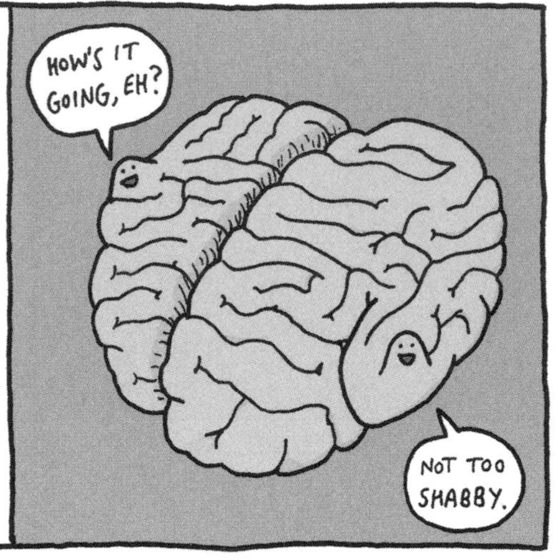

HOW'S IT GOING, EH?
NOT TOO SHABBY.

DANCING HELPS YOU BUILD THOSE BRAIN CONNECTIONS.
AND IT CAN EVEN HELP YOU HAVE A BETTER MEMORY.

REALLY?
YEP. IF I REMEMBER CORRECTLY.

GUS, WHY DO YOU KNOW SO MUCH ABOUT BRAINS?

OH! NO REASON. JUST A BIT OF HARMLESS BRAIN RESEARCH. HONEST!

YESSIR! COMPLETELY HARMLESS!

ENOUGH TALK! LET'S DANCE!

TRY IT!
DANCING IS EASY! I'LL SHOW YOU HOW!
FIRST, PUT ON SOME MUSIC. SOMETHING WITH A GOOD BEAT. THEN, TRY DOING THE STEPS THAT I'M GOING TO SHOW YOU.

FIRST, WE'LL WALK SIDEWAYS TO THE RIGHT...
STEP TO THE RIGHT.
THEN BRING OVER THE LEFT FOOT.
AND ANOTHER STEP TO THE RIGHT.
AND BRING OVER THE LEFT FOOT.

AND THEN WE WALK BACK TO THE LEFT...
STEP TO THE LEFT.
BRING OVER THE RIGHT FOOT.
AND ANOTHER STEP TO THE LEFT.
AND BRING THE RIGHT FOOT.

NOW TRY IT WITH A KICK AT THE END...
STEP TO THE RIGHT.
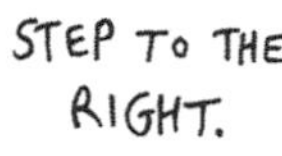

BRING OVER THE LEFT FOOT.

AND ANOTHER STEP RIGHT.

AND THEN KICK OUT WITH THE LEFT.

AND THEN BACK TO THE LEFT...

STEP TO THE LEFT.

BRING OVER THE RIGHT FOOT.

AND ANOTHER STEP TO THE LEFT.

THEN KICK WITH THE RIGHT FOOT.
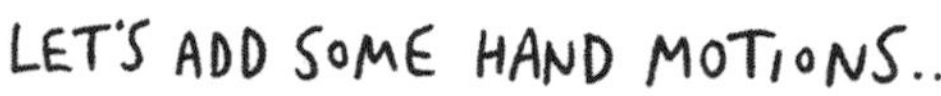
LET'S ADD SOME HAND MOTIONS...

STEP RIGHT, ARMS TO THE RIGHT.

BRING LEFT FOOT OVER ARMS LEFT.

STEP RIGHT, ARMS TO THE RIGHT.

KICK WITH LEFT FOOT, ARMS LEFT.

AND BACK AGAIN...
STEP LEFT. ARMS TO THE RIGHT.
BRING OVER RIGHT FOOT. ARMS LEFT.

ANOTHER STEP LEFT. ARMS TO THE RIGHT.

KICK OUT RIGHT FOOT. ARMS LEFT.

NOW LET'S GET FANCY. TRY THE "RIDE-A-BIKE"...
STEP RIGHT. PRETEND TO HOLD HANDLEBARS.
BRING OVER THE LEFT FOOT.
AND ANOTHER STEP TO THE RIGHT.

BRING OVER LEFT FOOT. STEER RIGHT.

AND NOW DO THE "LASER EYES"!
STEP LEFT. HOLD HANDS NEAR EYES.
BRING OVER RIGHT FOOT. SHOOT OUT ARMS.
ANOTHER STEP LEFT. HANDS NEAR EYES.

BRING OVER RIGHT FOOT AND ZZZT!

Andrews McMeel Publishing
a division of Andrews McMeel Universal
1130 Walnut Street, Kansas City, Missouri 64106

www.andrewsmcmeel.com
www.lasermooseandrabbitboy.com

17 18 19 20 21 RR2 10 9 8 7 6 5 4 3 2 1

ISBN: 978-1-4494-8687-7

Library of Congress Control Number: 2016957828

Made by:
LSC Communications US, LLC
Address and location of manufacturer:
1009 Sloan Street
Crawford, IN 47933
1st Printing – 9/15/17

Editor: Jean Z. Lucas
Designer: Spencer Williams
Art Director: Julie Barnes
Color Assistance: J.L. Martin
Production Manager: Chuck Harper
Production Editor: Maureen Sullivan
Demand Planner: Sue Eikos

Check out these and other books at ampkids.com

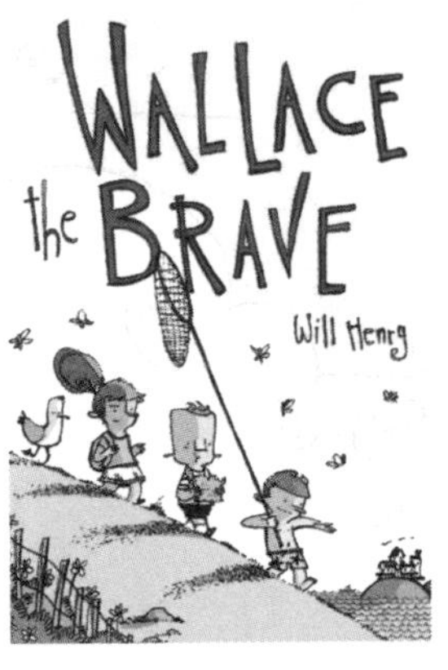

Also available:
Teaching and activity guides for each title.
AMP! Comics for Kids books make reading FUN!